DAVID MORTIMORE BAXTER

Wild!

by Karen Tayleur

illustrated by Brann Garvey

Librarian Reviewer
Laurie K. Holland
Media Specialist (National Board Certified), Edina, MN
MA in Elementary Education, Minnesota State University, Mankato

Reading Consultant
Elizabeth Stedem
Educator/Consultant, Colorado Springs, CO
MA in Elementary Education, University of Denver, CO

 STONE ARCH BOOKS
Minneapolis   San Diego

David Mortimore Baxter is published by Stone Arch Books
151 Good Counsel Drive, P.O. Box 669
Mankato, Minnesota 56002
www.stonearchbooks.com

Text copyright © 2008 Karen Tayleur
Copyright © 2008 Stone Arch Books

Library of Congress Cataloging-in-Publication Data
Tayleur, Karen.
    Wild!: Get Lost with David Mortimore Baxter / by Karen Tayleur; illustrated
by Brann Garvey.
        p. cm. — (David Mortimore Baxter)
    ISBN 978-1-4342-0463-9 (library binding)
    ISBN 978-1-4342-0513-1 (paperback)
    [1. Lost children—Fiction. 2. Humorous stories.] I. Garvey, Brann, ill.
II. Title.
PZ7.T21149Wil 2008
[Fic]—dc22   2007030745

Summary: David's dad makes an announcement one day: The Baxters are going
camping over spring break. David can't believe it! Who wants to sleep on the
ground in the woods when you could be snoozing in your own bed? But Mr. Baxter
insists. Luckily, Joe and Bec, David's best friends, are going too. But when David is
left in charge of his little brother, things go from bad to worse. The only thing that
could make this trip more of a disaster would be if the three friends got lost in the
wild. But David is too smart for that, right?

Art Director: Heather Kindseth
Graphic Designer: Kay Fraser

Photo Credits
Delaney Photography, cover

1 2 3 4 5 6 13 12 11 10 09 08

Printed in the United States of America

Table of Contents

CHAPTER 1

GETTING LOST

It was all Harry's fault.

I checked my watch. It had been over two hours. **I felt sick.**

If only Dad hadn't needed to go to town.

If only **Bec** and **Joe** hadn't come camping with us. Then there would have been room in one car for *everyone* to go into town.

If only Mom and Dad hadn't left me in charge of Harry.

Now Harry was lost.

If Mom and Dad didn't ground me for the rest of my life when they found out I lost their child, then my name wasn't **David Mortimore Baxter.**

> HELLO
> MY NAME IS
> DAVID MORTIMORE
> BAXTER

"Harry," I called out in my loudest voice. "𝓗𝓐𝓐𝓐𝓐𝓐𝓡𝓡𝓡𝓡𝓡𝓡𝓡𝓨."

My backpack straps were digging into my shoulders.

A trickle of sweat was inching down between my shoulder blades. I was so *uncomfortable*. All I could think about was my air bed back at camp.

How could such a fun vacation turn into such a disaster?

My best friends, Bec and Joe, were talking loudly. I heard something moving in the trees.

I held up my hand. "**Quiet**," I said. "Did you hear that?"

We stood still and listened. Something was CRASHING through the trees. Was it Harry? Or was it *something else*?

"Harry?" **Joe** called.

We heard more noise in the trees nearby.

"If it was Harry, he'd answer us, wouldn't he?" asked Bec.

"So what are you trying to say?" said Joe.

"She's saying that she doesn't think Harry is making that noise," I answered.

I thought about all the things it **could** be.

I wasn't quite sure what wild animals lived around here. Dad had said something about **bears**.

Maybe there were bears. Bears with huge, pointy teeth and long, sharp claws.

Or maybe it was the **hermit fisherman** out for REVENGE.

Harry Archibald Baxter was in **big trouble**. If he was still alive by the time I found him, **I was going to kill him.**

Not only had I lost Harry, but I had now put my two best friends in DANGER. Today was the worst day of my entire life.

"I think we should move away from the path," I said. "Something's following us. We need to get some cover."

"I don't know, David," said Bec.

Joe nodded. "You're right, David. We're **sitting ducks** here."

"Let's go," I said. I didn't wait to see if Bec was going to follow me.

I headed off into the thick forest that surrounded us. I thought about the things I had in my backpack. There was nothing to use as a weapon against a wild animal. **My bug spray wasn't going to do much.**

I looked back. Bec and Joe were following, heads down, behind me. We walked for about fifteen minutes without talking.

Then Joe called out. He was standing in front of a tree that was leaning to one side like **it might fall over any minute.**

"What is it?" I asked.

Joe was waving a piece of red faded plastic at me. It had some yellow letters printed on it. "Is this Harry's?" he asked.

"That plastic has been here **since the dinosaurs,**" snapped Bec.

"Let's just keep going," I said.

"David, we should dig a trap, just in case that thing tries to 𝔽𝕆𝕃𝕃𝕆𝕎 us," said Joe.

"A trap?" I asked.

"Yeah, you know, like that movie I told you about. The one I watched the other night," Joe said.

Joe once tried to make a list of movies that he'd seen, but when we ran out of paper he had to stop. **Joe has seen more movies than anyone in the world.** It helps that his parents own a video store.

"Not another movie," said Bec, groaning.

"No, this could help," said Joe. "These people were in a jungle being **hunted** by a group of murderers."

"This isn't a jungle," interrupted Bec.

"Also, we should be careful not to walk through the streams, just in case," Joe said.

"In case of what?" asked Bec.

"Piranhas," said Joe. "They are these really awful fish with sharp teeth. *They can gobble up a human in ten seconds.*"

"I don't think we have any **piranhas** in this country," I said.

"Can you be sure of that?" asked Joe. "Maybe you could go across the stream first."

I shook my head. "There is no stream here, Joe," I told him. Then I turned around and kept walking.

Soon, Joe stopped talking about **deadly fish that ate humans.**

All I could hear was the crunch of our feet as we walked over leaves and twigs.

I guess I wasn't paying too much attention to what I was doing. I was trying to think of a good excuse to tell Mom and Dad when they asked me how I **lost** my **brother.**

Then Joe said, "Hey, look at this." Joe was holding up a faded piece of red plastic.

"Another piece of plastic," said Bec, shaking her head.

I squinted at the plastic. "I don't think so," I said.

"What do you mean, David?" Bec asked.

"Did you get rid of that first piece, Joe?" I asked.

Joe nodded. He held it up and I could see the letters, printed in yellow.

"It's the same piece," I said.

I *pointed* to a tree that was leaning over so far it looked like it might FALL OVER.

"I think I've seen that tree before," I said.

"We've been walking in **circles**," said Joe.

I nodded again. **"We're lost."**

CHAPTER 2

COULD HAVE, SHOULD HAVE, DIDN'T

Every year during spring break, my family goes on vacation to the beach. **Every year, it is the same thing.** I like it that way.

This year, Dad wanted to do something *different.*

One Sunday, my best friends, Joe and Bec came over for lunch. Suddenly, Dad said, "I think we should go CAMPING this year during spring break."

"But we always go to the beach," I complained.

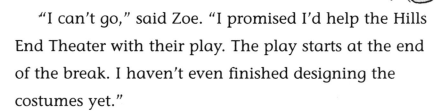

"That's my point," said **Dad.** "This year, I *want a change.* I want to go camping."

"I can't go," said Zoe. "I promised I'd help the Hills End Theater with their play. The play starts at the end of the break. I haven't even finished designing the costumes yet."

"But you can't stay here **alone**," said Dad.

Joe, Bec, and Gran stayed quiet as they watched **Zoe** go into **danger mode.**

"You treat me like I'm a **baby**," Zoe said, pushing her chair away from the table and standing up. She raised her head high and added, "I think you should know that Ally Bohmer stayed home for four weeks by herself while her parents went to Switzerland last year."

"How **irresponsible** of them," said **Mom**.

"And Laura Day's mother travels a lot for her job. A lot. And you don't see her say Laura's too young to be home alone," continued Zoe.

"Is Laura that girl with the **tattoo on her neck?**" asked Harry.

Zoe ignored Harry and went on. "I hate camping. Mom, he can't make us go, can he?" Zoe was crying. **Big, fat tears** made her makeup all 𝕊𝕄𝔼𝔸ℝ𝕐.

"We'll discuss this later," said Mom.  "Anyone want more mashed potatoes?"

"She can stay with me," said **Gran** suddenly. We all stared at her.

"Now, Mother," said Dad.

Gran said, "Thomas, you cannot make that girl go camping. **She'll hate it.** Look at her. That's not a person who should sleep in a tent on the ground."

Zoe had stopped CRYING and was staring at Gran.

"I know you and your father loved camping, Thomas," continued Gran, "but I always thought it was DISGUSTING. What is the point of sleeping outside in the wilderness?"

"Now, Mother," Dad repeated.

"What do you say?" Gran asked Zoe.

"Yes," said Zoe quickly. "Yes!"

"I think camping's **cool**," said Joe.

Then everyone started talking at the same time. It got really loud.

Mom wanted to know *where we would go.*

Dad talked about **tents.**

Harry kept saying how **great** it was going to be.

Joe kept repeating that he thought camping was COOL.

Then it was decided. Zoe would stay with Gran. The rest of the family, plus Joe and Bec, would go camping.

"Only if that's okay with your parents," said Dad to Joe and Bec.

"But that means we'll have to  take two cars," said Harry.

"We're going to need two cars anyway," said Dad. *"We have to pack a lot of stuff."*

"And **Boris**," I said. "Boris has to come too. He can't stay home alone."

Then Mom wanted to know how she was going to cook, and how long we were going for, and **would we be able to take baths.**

"It's going to be great," said Dad. "I used to go camping all the time when I was a kid. There's nothing like it. Fresh air. The smell of food cooking on the campfire. Fishing in a stream. **No TVs**. No work. **Just being at one with nature."**

"What?" said Harry. "No TV?"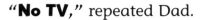

"No TV," repeated Dad.

"Who's cooking on the campfire?" asked Mom.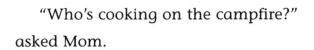

"I am," said Dad.

"Well, that's fine then," said Mom.

"This is going to be cool, David," said Joe.

But I wasn't so sure.

CHAPTER 3

OPERATION: CAMPING

Dad was **really excited** about camping. The week before we left, he went to Gran's house to get all his old camping gear. He laid everything out in our back yard and asked Harry and me to help him.

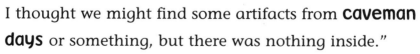

"This is going to be great, boys," he said. "You're going to love it. I was a Boy Scout when I was your age, and I did a lot of camping."

"I guess *they didn't have* TV back then," Harry whispered to me.

"There wasn't much to do," I agreed.

"My father and I LOVED camping," said **Dad**. "One year we found an amazing cave. It went on for miles underground. I thought we might find some artifacts from **caveman days** or something, but there was nothing inside."

"What if you had found something, Dad?" asked Harry.

"I guess we'd have to give it to a museum," said Dad thoughtfully. "Or the government or something."

Then Harry stood on a tent pole by mistake and Dad got bossier than usual.

Dad's Rules

1. Don't stand on the tent.

2. Don't play with the hammer.

3. Keep the dog away.

If this was what camping was going to be like, I HATED it already.

The tent was a huge canvas square. I stood at one corner of the tent and Harry stood at another.

Dad hammered some pegs through loops in the bottom of the tent. That was to keep the tent in place. Then he grabbed a long wooden pole.

"Now, just follow my instructions," said Dad, "and this will be up in a second."

Half an hour later, Harry and I were still standing at our corners.

First, Dad couldn't find the pole that went through the tent roof. Then, he couldn't find the ropes that helped tie the tent down to the ground.

One of the side poles was **so old** it cracked in ᕼᗩᒪᖴ when Dad tried to use it, so he had to tape it together.

Putting up a tent always looked so easy in the movies.

Finally, Harry and I let go of our poles. The tent didn't fall down.

"Come inside," said Dad.

Inside the tent, **the light was all green**. Maybe it was because of the green roof. Tiny pinpricks of light were shining through the roof.

"There are holes in the roof," I told Dad.

Dad squinted. "That's just the canvas," he explained. "The canvas needs to ᗷᖇᕮᗩᔕ. That keeps you from getting **too hot** in the tent."

"The canvas breathes?" said Harry.

"Well, not really ᗷᖇᕮᗩᔕᕼᕮᔕ," said Dad. "It lets the air in. And out."

"Are you sure they're not 𝐇𝐎𝐋𝐄𝐒?" I asked.

Now that the tent was up, it seemed small to me. I couldn't imagine us all fitting in it.

Harry wanted to know what we were sleeping on. *He thought we were going to bring our regular beds,* and he was worried there wouldn't be room in the car for all of those beds.

Dad explained we'd be using air beds instead. He said we would put our sleeping bags on top of the air beds.

That sounded pretty comfortable. I always thought camping meant **sleeping on the ground**.

Then Joe and Bec came over. They headed into the back yard to check out the tent.

"I think I see 𝐇𝐎𝐋𝐄𝐒 in the roof," Joe said.

"I'm bringing **my own** tent," said Bec. "Actually, it's my sister's. She got it last year for her school campout."

"Maybe all three of us could sleep in that," said Joe.

Bec shook her head. "It's a **single** tent," she explained. "Anyway, I like to read late at night, so I don't want to keep anyone awake."

"Well, Mom said I could borrow my cousin's tent," said Joe. "It's one of those **cool space dome tents** that they use in the snow. It fits two people. We could sleep in that, David."

"Sure," I said.

I told Dad that Bec and Joe were bringing their own tents. His face turned SERIOUS and he crossed his arms.

"I'll need to **inspect** those tents," he said. "I like to make sure all my equipment is in good working order before I go anywhere."

Inspect?

Ever since we decided to go on the camping trip, **Dad had been acting really strange.** He'd started speaking in army talk, like saying **"oh eight hundred hours"** instead of "eight o'clock in the morning." He'd also asked Mom if she had her equipment for the mess tent ready.

Mom asked him *what messy tent*. Then Dad explained that he was talking about a tent where we prepared and ate our rations.

"Rations? You mean food?" asked Mom.

"Yes," said Dad.

Joe and Bec brought their tents over the next day. Bec's was a **tiny orange tent** that had just enough room for her and her backpack.

"Now, let's see you put that up," said Dad. "Unless you want help."

"I can do it," said Bec.

She looked at our big canvas tent that was still up in the back yard. Then she took out her tent.

She put in the pegs, stuck in the poles, and put another piece of canvas over the top.

It only took her ten minutes.

Joe and I had planned to put up our tent together, but Dad was already ripping the tent out of its bag and pulling out some black plastic rods.

He spread the pieces out on the ground.

"Would anyone like **something to eat**?" Mom called out from the back door.

Joe, Bec, and I ran inside, but Dad stayed outside.

"I'll just be a moment," said Dad.

The three of us ate some cake. Then we watched our favorite game show, "SLIME THAT KID." About an hour later, I realized that Dad was still outside.

We ran out and saw that Joe's tent was just a puddle of plastic on the grass.

Dad was laying the long black poles on the grass and measuring each one.

"Almost there," he said cheerfully.

He was still working on it when I went to bed that night.

CHAPTER 4

ARTY FACTS

Everyone at school was excited about spring break. There were only three days to go before break, and you could feel the 𝓗𝓐𝓟𝓟𝓘𝓝𝓔𝓢𝓢 and **excitement** in the air. Even the teachers looked less annoyed than they usually did.

Everyone had a plan for their vacation. Before class started, we talked about what we were going to do.

Jake Davern was going to visit the **zoo** during his vacation.

Sam Beavis was going to the **Football Hall of Fame** with his uncle, who worked there.

Paul Jurkovic said his dad was going to take him **surfing**.

Rose Thornton kept telling people that she couldn't tell anyone where she was going for her vacation.

"Fine," said Joe. "I don't want to know."

"Don't try to trick me, Joe Pagnopolous," said Rose. "I couldn't even tell you if I wanted to. Which I don't."

"Fine," said Joe.

Rose glared at me. "And I'm definitely not telling you, David."

"**Whatever**," I said, shrugging. "But why can't you tell us?"

"It's a SURPRISE," said Rose. "Mother won't tell me. But I think it might be **Paris**. I saw her getting out our suitcases the other night."

"Paris!" said Bec. **"Paris, France?"**

"Shhhhh," said Rose. "Not so loud. I'm only guessing. Maybe it's **Hawaii**, but we went there last year. I can't wait to find out."

"Well, we're going somewhere too," I said. "But I'm not telling you where."

"You are?" said Rose. "Where?"

"CAMPING," said **Joe,** smiling widely.

"Joe!" said Bec.

"Hey!" I said. I punched his arm.

Joe looked shocked. "I told her what we're doing, but she doesn't know we're going to *Blue Hill State Park!*" he whispered loudly.

Rose LAUGHED.

Bec SIGHED.

I punched Joe's arm again.

"Camping!" said Rose. "How disgusting! All that dirt. All those **creepy crawlies.**" She shivered.

"Gee, Rose," I said. "You should be used to creepy things."

"**Are you saying I'm creepy**, David Baxter?" she shrieked.

Just then, **Ms. Stacey**, our teacher, came into the room. Everyone went to their seats.

She thumped her books down on her desk like normal, but she was *smiling*. She pulled out a piece of newspaper and gave it to Jake.

"Pass that around, please, Jake," Ms. Stacey said.

Then Ms. Stacey went to the board and wrote the word **"artifact."**

"Does anyone know what this word means?" she asked.

"Is it art that is a fact?" asked Alysha Devine.

"No," said Ms. Stacey. "But good try. Anyone else?"

"Is it a vegetable?" asked Joe.

"No," said Ms. Stacey. "Maybe you're thinking of **artichoke**."

"Is it a bunch of old stuff?" asked Chris.

Ms. Stacey scratched her head and said, "Something like that. I would like you all to copy down the definition of **artifact** from the board."

artifact (ART-uh-fakt) — a human-made object that was used in an ancient time.

"Now, can anyone give me an example of an artifact?" asked Ms. Stacey.

"A video tape?" said Jake.

"The Broncos' old uniforms?" said Sam.

I remembered Dad telling us about finding a cave one camping trip.

"Stuff leftover from cavemen?" I said.

"Right, David," said Ms. Stacey.

She looked surprised like she always does when I do something right.

Then she talked about the **pyramids** and how they were built for the ancient Egyptian kings. She said that the pyramids were filled with all sorts of things like **jewelry, furniture, and even games.**

Joe asked me what kind of game I thought I'd take with me into a pyramid.

I was still thinking about it when Rose raised her hand. I hate it when she does that. Bec looked at me and **rolled her eyes.**

"Yes, Rose," said Ms. Stacey.

"I've been to the pyramids," said Rose.

"Really? How wonderful," said Ms. Stacey.

Rose had the look on her face that always makes me mad.

"We went on a guided tour," continued Rose. "It was **incredibly** hot. I wasn't feeling well. Mother said I must have had heat stroke. Afterward, I took a very long nap."

"Ohhhhh," cooed Rose's friends.

I couldn't stand it. "Well, **my dad found some artifacts in a cave** when he was a kid," I **said loudly**.

That wasn't exactly true. Dad had told us that he had found a cave. There hadn't been anything inside the cave, but *maybe he just hadn't looked hard enough.*

"Really?" said Ms. Stacey. "What did he find?"

"Oh, you know," I said.

Joe poked me in the ribs. I know he wanted me to stop talking, but Rose was looking at me and waiting for me to back down.

"Some tools," I said.

"What sort of tools?" demanded Rose.

"**Arrowheads**," I said.

"Really?" said Ms. Stacey. **"Could you bring them in?"**

I shook my head. "No. He had to give them to a **museum**. So they aren't at our house, because they're at the museum."

Rose asked me what museum, but I pretended I didn't hear her.

Then Ms. Stacey talked some more about the article she'd clipped out of the newspaper that morning. In the article, it said that someone had found some really old paintings on cave walls.

"Older than my dad?" asked Jake.

"Even older than that," Ms. Stacey agreed.

"Wouldn't it be COOL if we found some artifacts when we go camping?" whispered Joe.

"WAY COOL," I said.

But I was just happy that everyone had forgotten about Rose Thornton and her stupid trip to the pyramids. Rose always gets so much attention, and I can't stand it.

Then Rose walked past my desk to put something into the trash. On the way back she hissed, **"Liar!"**

I'll show you, Rose Thornton, I thought. **I'll show you.**

CHAPTER 5

DESTINATION: BLUE HILLS

We left for our camping trip on Friday after school. Zoe had already left to stay at Gran's. **Boris** was walking around and getting under everyone's feet.

"Can someone please *take that dog outside?*" Mom kept saying. But no one did.

Bec and Joe were helping us take stuff out to the cars. We had **a lot** of stuff.

There were tents, sleeping bags, pillows, air beds, lanterns, folding chairs, a camp stove, a frying pan, plastic plates, silverware, tin mugs, three fishing rods, towels, soap, and a game of Monopoly.

And lots more.

"This isn't going to fit," said Mom.

"Sure it will," said Dad.

No one was allowed to pack the cars except Dad. We had to bring the stuff out to the front lawn. Then Dad went through his list and checked things off. He made sure we had everything.

Mr. McCafferty, who happened to be walking past, stopped to watch. He and Dad talked about the trip and where we were going and how long it should take and *whether we had enough gas in the car.*

Mr. McCafferty promised to keep an eye on our house. He was going to collect the mail while we were gone.

"Thanks," said Dad.

Mr. McCafferty waved.

"Maybe we should have invited him to come camping with us," said Dad.

"Just keep packing," said Mom.

We were supposed to leave at 1620 hours (4:20 p.m.) but in the end we didn't leave until 1800 hours (6 p.m.).

Dad, Harry, and Boris were in Dad's car. **They led the way.** I sat in the front of Mom's car. Joe and Bec sat in the back.

Mom hated having to follow Dad, but she didn't know how to get to the state park.

We'd only been driving for half an hour when Dad stopped at a gas station.

Harry had to go to the bathroom. Dad put some gas in the car. Bec, Joe, and I bought some **candy.** Then we waved to Boris, who was sleeping on the floor in the back of Dad's car.

"He doesn't look very happy," said Bec.

"He always looks like that," I said. "I think he's okay."

Then Dad was ready to go. We all jumped back in our cars and drove off again.

Fifteen minutes later, Dad stopped the car and we stopped behind him. He got out of the car, checked the strapping on his roof rack, then got back in and drove off again.

"This is going to be a very LONG TRIP," said Mom.

Finally, after we stopped at least five more times, Dad turned at a big sign.

The sign said **"Blue Hill State Park."**

Near the entrance was the ranger's hut, but there were no lights on. I guess it was too late for anyone to be awake.

We followed Dad down a nice smooth road, then down another bumpier road, then down a really bumpy path.

"I hope your father knows where he's going," said Mom.

Suddenly, Dad's brake lights glowed red in the dark and the car stopped. There was a lot of **yelling and cheering** from Harry and Dad in the car in front.

"Are we here?" said Bec.

"Looks like it," I said.

We got out of the car. Mom kept the headlights on so we could see.

We walked around Dad's car and found ourselves in a campsite. There was a ring of stones that might have once been a campfire.

Dad looked **pretty pleased** with himself.

"Wait," he said.

Then he went to the car and got a plastic sheet out. He spread it on the ground and told us to lie on it and **look up at the sky.**

"Trust me," said Dad.

So we all lay on the sheet, even Boris, who seemed happy to be out of the car. Then Dad went back to the cars to turn off the headlights.

"Close your eyes until I tell you," he ordered.

I heard first one car door SLAM, then another, then the CRUNCH of Dad's footsteps as he came back to us.

"Open your eyes," he commanded.

"Wow!" said Joe.

"Cool," said Harry.

"Oh, Thomas," said Mom.

It was AMAZING. I always thought the night sky at home was cool, but it wasn't really.

Way above us was an inky dome dotted with bright jewels.

There were way more stars than I ever knew existed. As we watched, a light streaked across the sky.

"What was that?" said Harry.

"That," said Dad, "was **a shooting star.** Did you make a wish?"

"I wish we could stay here forever," said Harry.

Later, when I was running through the trees looking for my brother, I was hoping that **his wish would not come true.**

CHAPTER 6

A STRANGER IN THE TENT

We set up our tents in the light of Dad's car.

Dad just wanted to set up one tent for the night, but Joe, Bec, and I wanted to set up our own tents.

Mom said, "Oh, let them, Thomas." So Dad just WAVED us away.

I helped Bec set her tent up while Joe pointed the flashlight our way.

Then Bec held the flashlight for Joe and me while we set up the dome tent. It was *pretty easy* to do, once we figured out where the door was supposed to go.

Meanwhile, Dad was ordering Mom around, trying to set up their tent. **Harry was running all over and not helping at all.**

Dad kept snapping orders and Mom and Harry tried to follow his directions, but you could tell *things were going to get nasty.*

"Let's blow up our air beds," I said.

So Bec, Joe, and I looked for the air pump.

"Where do you think it is?" asked Joe, as we poked around in the back of Dad's car.

"It should have been on top," I said. "Dad wanted all the camping stuff to be at the top."

"Maybe I should ask your dad," said Joe.

I looked over at the canvas tent that was still lying on the ground.

"Let's just **blow them up,**" I said.

It took forever to blow up the beds. The hardest thing was putting the plug into the hole **before all the air whooshed out.**

Joe and Bec were having a race to see who could blow up their bed first. Then **Joe** said he was 𝒟𝓘𝒵𝒵𝒴.

Bec told him to take some deep breaths and put his head between his knees. *She won the competition,* and then Joe had to lie down while Bec finished blowing up his bed.

Meanwhile, Dad was still trying to get his tent up.

Mom was busy. She was unpacking the cars.

Harry was holding one of the tent poles. He looked like he might fall asleep.

Dad's face was bright red.

I took a deep breath. I could see what I had to do. "Do you want some help, Dad?" I asked.

Dad nodded. So Joe, Bec, and I helped put the canvas tent up. It only took ten minutes and we CHEERED when we were done. Dad looked **proud,** like he'd done it all by himself.

Mom came to look at the tent and agreed that **we'd all done a wonderful job.** Then she shoved some sleeping bags at us and said we couldn't really do much more until daylight.

We couldn't find our clothes bags. Dad had packed them somewhere, underneath everything else.

"That's okay," said Joe. "We can sleep in our clothes. Then when we get up in the morning we're already dressed. Where's the bathroom?"

Dad explained that we were camping and *there was no bathroom.*

Then he handed Joe a small shovel, a roll of toilet paper, and a flashlight. **Dad explained about digging a hole and then covering up whatever you had put in the hole.**

"*HA HA*! But really, Mr. Baxter, where is the bathroom?" Joe asked.

When **Joe** found out Dad wasn't joking, he said that **he wasn't going to the bathroom until he could use a real one.**

"Joe, if you think you can hang on for **five days,** go right ahead," said Dad.

Bec got into her tent and settled down to do some reading.

"If you get scared in the night, just give our special *Secret Club* call," Joe told Bec.

Bec snorted. "I'll remember that," she said.

Joe and I took a flashlight and hopped into our sleeping bags in our tent.

Boris THUMPED down in front of the  tent on a sleeping bag cover.

I could hear Dad looking around for the air pump. Then he had a **discussion** with Mom about someone moving the pump.

Then Mom said that maybe he hadn't packed the pump, but Dad said it was marked off on his list, so it must be packed.

Then it got quiet and I heard the **plop plop plop** of something hitting the tent.

"It's raining," said Joe.

"Mmmm," I said. It sounded nice.

I must have fallen asleep, because the next thing I knew, my eyes were open, the light in the tent was gray instead of black, and **Joe was kicking me.**

"What?" I mumbled.

"You were SNORING," said Joe.

"I don't snore," I told him.

"Yep, you do," said Joe. "You've been snoring for the last hour. You woke me up."

I buried my head in my pillow. **It was way too early to be awake.**

Joe kicked me again. "You're doing it again," he said.

"What?" I said.

"Snoring," he said.

"I can't be snoring. **I'm awake,**" I said.

Then I heard it. A SNORE.

"*Sssshhhhh,*" I said.

We listened. There it was again. A long, deep snore. It was coming from inside the tent.

"That's not you, is it, Joe?" I asked.

"No," said Joe.

"Then something else is in our tent," I told him.

"What?" whispered Joe. "What could it be?"

I was thinking about what might sneak into our tent in the middle of the night and start snoring. **I thought about bears** and pulled my knees up under my chin.

I wondered if bears liked feet. **Maybe just toes.**

I looked around for the flashlight. Finally, I found it under my pillow, exactly where I'd put it before I went to sleep. I shined it around the tent.

Finally, I found the problem near our tent's doorway.

The zipper was slightly open and **a large head was poking through.**

It was Boris.

CHAPTER 7

BE PREPARED

I must have fallen asleep again, because the next thing I knew it really was morning.

I could hear the $\mathbb{SIZZLE}$ of something frying not far away. The smell of bacon was floating into our tent and making Boris *slobber* in his sleep.

Joe was still asleep. I shook his shoulder.

"Mmmmpph?" said Joe.

"Come on," I said. **"Get up."**

Dad was cooking outside. He smiled when Joe and I stepped out of our tent. "Good morning, boys," he said. "Sleep well?"

Harry was up too. He was putting sticks into the fire. "It rained last night. **We got wet**," he said, cheerfully.

"Did the rain come through the **breathing holes**?" I asked.

Dad scraped at the food in the frying pan. "That's one of today's jobs," he said. "I'll have to take a look at that roof. Luckily, I have a patch kit with me. I was a Boy Scout, you know. And you know the Boy Scout motto."

"A patch a day keeps you dry?" said Joe.

"Be prepared," said Dad.

"I think **your bacon's on fire**, Dad," I told him. Flames were shooting up into the air from the frying pan.

Dad was running around and trying to keep us away when Harry popped a saucepan lid on top of it.

"We learned that at school," said Harry.

"Good job, son," said Dad. "Looks like we'll need some more bacon, though."

"Is something burning out there?" said Mom from inside the canvas tent.

"Everything's under control, Cordelia," said Dad, making faces at us. "Boris, looks like **you get breakfast first.**"

Boris opened one eye and then shut  it again.

Joe and I set up some chairs around the fire and waited with our plates for the next round of bacon.

Then Bec and Mom came out of their tents and **we feasted on bacon and eggs and bread** that was toasted over the fire.

"This is the life," said Dad, as he sat back in his chair.

We all agreed and sat back in our own chairs.

After a few minutes, Harry said, "So what are we going to do next, Dad?"

"We need to set up camp properly," said Dad. "There are **chores** to be done. You need to SWEEP out the tents to keep the dirt out. We need to dry out some of the bedding."

"Chores?" I said. "What do you mean, chores? We're not at home."

"And we need to **organize** the mess tent. I suppose I should dig a trench around the tents in case it rains again," continued Dad.

"Don't you think it's a little late for that?" asked Mom.

"Remember the Boy Scout motto," said Dad.

"Be prepared!" I said.

"Thomas, you are too old to be a Boy Scout. And **I did not come on this vacation to work.** I'm going for a walk. Would anyone like to come with me?" asked Mom.

Everyone except Dad said yes. He was too busy washing the dishes in a little plastic tub.

"Are you using our drinking water?" asked Mom.

"No," said Dad. "There's water nearby. I'll just stay here and do the dishes."

"They'll still be here when we come back," said Mom.

"They'd be full of bugs," said Dad. "That's all right. You go. I'll go next time."

I got the feeling that Dad wanted us to stay and help him.

I left **Boris** with him instead.

"Stay, boy," I said.

I don't know why I bothered. **Boris wasn't going anywhere.** He was lying down near the small fire, sniffing for bacon pieces in the dirt.

"Good boy," I said. **"Good dog."** Then we took off on our hike.

Mom led us down a trail through the trees.

Every now and then we'd stop and look at a huge **spider web** strung out between some bushes, or a forgotten **bird's nest,** or **mushrooms.**

Suddenly, the trees cleared and we were standing on a small hill. We could hear rushing water.

"A **RIVER!**" said Harry. He started taking his shoes off.

We rushed down to the water's edge. It wasn't really a river. It was more of a stream. The water was clear and you could see large river pebbles on the bottom.

Harry poked his toe in the water and pulled it out again. **"Freezing,"** he said.

"I'm not surprised," said Mom. "You're used to the pool."

I grabbed some flat pebbles from the water's edge and started skipping them across the top of the water. It was easier than **skipping rocks at the beach.** The water was flat and smooth and the pebble skipped four times across the surface before dropping to the bottom.

"Hey, **how do you do that?**" asked Joe.

"Show me first," said Bec.

We spent the next 20 minutes skipping rocks. After a few minutes, Mom went back to camp and said we shouldn't wander off. I think *she was feeling guilty* about leaving Dad alone with Boris and the dirty dishes.

We were having a pretty peaceful morning. Then Harry dropped a 𝓗𝓤𝓖𝓔 𝓡𝓞𝓒𝓚 right in the middle of the stream.

"**Hey! Cut that out,**" a voice rang out from the trees on the opposite bank. There was a flash of color through the trees, but I couldn't see anyone.

Then I spied it. Sunlight glinted on a thin fishing line that had been cast out from the other side of the stream.

"This is **private property**," said the voice. "You're **trespassing**."

"This is a state park," said Bec.

There was silence. I wondered how old the fisherman was. It was hard to tell from his voice.

"Well, you have no right," he said finally. "You are SCARING the fish away."

"Sorry," said Joe. "So are there fish here?"

The person didn't say anything, but I could hear the click click of the reel as he wound the line in.

"Okay, we'll stop," Harry yelled.

"I think he's **annoyed** that you're making too much noise," I said.

"Stay away from here, if you know what's good for you," came the voice again.

Then there was the sound of twigs breaking as the fisherman walked away.

CHAPTER 8

TRESPASSING

Back at camp, **Dad had been busy.**
There was another tent set up on the edge of camp.
Dad said this was the mess tent. It just looked like any
other tent to me except that it was very, very blue.

"Where did that come from?" I asked.

"It was really CHEAP," said Dad, flicking an
insect off the bright blue tent. "They were having a
sale at Tent World."

"It's **very blue**," said Bec.

"Probably why it was on sale," I muttered.

"Come and have a look," said Dad.

We walked into the blue tent. Dad had
stacked the tubs of food and two car fridges
to one side. On another side was a small table.

"That's the **preparation table**," said Dad.

"Preparation for what?" said Joe.

"That's where our meals will be made," said Dad.

Then he pointed underneath and showed us where the plastic plates, silverware, and cups were. On the back wall of the tent was a small table with chairs.

Dad seemed to be waiting for us to say something, so we all said how great it looked.

"Let's play Monopoly," said Joe.

Joe was as bad as Dad. We were camping. Weren't we supposed to be doing outside stuff, not *making another house* and playing a board game?

"Okay," said Bec.

"Can I be the banker?" asked Harry.

We played on the table in the mess tent. It was pretty cool sitting in a blue tent playing Monopoly, knowing there was just a thin wall of plastic (or whatever the blue tent was made out of) between **you** and **the wild.**

Even though Mom had said Dad would be doing all the cooking, **she couldn't help herself.** She made lots of noise at the preparation table, leaning over every now and then to help Harry be the banker.

Dad kept coming in and out looking very important and busy. I wasn't sure what he was doing, but he was having fun.

Mom cooked something she called **griddle cakes.** They were actually *really good*. She cooked them in the frying pan over the low fire that Dad had kept burning after breakfast.

We had them HOT and smeared with butter. I couldn't believe I was hungry after such a big breakfast, but I managed to eat five and Joe had six of the DELICIOUS cakes.

"How did you learn to make those?" asked Dad.

"A good chef never tells her secrets," said Mom.

After we got tired of playing Monopoly, Dad decided we should go for a walk.

"Let's stretch our legs," he said. **"Get some of that fresh air into our lungs."**

"Maybe I should stay and take care of the campsite," said Joe. He was eyeing the last griddle cake.

"Boris is on guard," said Dad. "I'll lock up the cars."

Dad took a backpack with some water bottles, just in case we got **thirsty**. Then he led the way. Mom and Harry were the last ones in line and Joe, Bec, and I were in the middle.

We took the **trail** back down to the stream. Then we turned onto another path that followed another stream. Dad told us that he and Grandpa used to come here a lot when Dad was just a kid. **It was strange to think of Dad as a kid.**

Dad seemed to have somewhere in mind, the way he was walking. My feet were starting to hurt and Joe's face was looking **redder than a bottle of ketchup.**

"Are we almost there?" complained Harry from the back of the line.

And then we were.

Dad turned to the left and stopped dead. The rest of us almost crashed into him.

"What is it, Dad?" I asked.

Dad was shaking his head like he couldn't believe something. "It's gone," was all he could say. He pointed to a pile of rocks.

Apparently Dad's big surprise was his secret cave, and it had been blocked off. *Dad seemed so sad that I thought he might cry.* Mom patted him on the shoulder and said that she didn't like caves anyway and maybe we should get back to camp and think about lunch.

On the way back to camp, Dad taught us a song about knapsacks being on our backs. Harry wanted to know what a knapsack was and Dad said it didn't matter what a knapsack was, just sing. We sang all the way past the stream and cracked up laughing when **Harry almost fell in.** We were still laughing when we walked back into camp.

Dad stopped dead for the second time that day and dropped his backpack.

All the chairs had been knocked over.

The frying pan that Mom had used for the griddle cakes was lying in the dirt.

The poles from Bec's tent had been knocked out, so it was just an orange puddle on the ground.

The mess tent was looking very messy. One side of the tent was leaning into the middle. It looked like a pole had been bent.

Dad walked over to the mess tent and looked inside. "OH!" he groaned.

We followed him in. The plates and cups were under the preparation table, knocked over. The Monopoly set was on the floor and the money was everywhere. Food was scattered all over.

"Now that's a messy tent," said Harry.

"That . . . THAT DOG!" said Dad.

"No!" I yelled. I couldn't believe he'd blame Boris. Boris would never have enough energy to do that kind of damage.

"Well, what else could have done this?" said Mom. "It wasn't the wind."

I went outside and found Boris asleep near the fire where we'd left him. It looked like he hadn't moved.

"Tie that dog up," said Dad angrily. "He's a menace."

I looked at Boris. "Did you do this, Boris?" I asked.

Boris just opened one eye and closed it again.

"I can't believe Boris did that," said Joe, giving Boris a pat.

"I can't either," said Bec.

"But what else—" I began.

"You mean **who else**?" said Bec.

"But there is no one else around here," said Joe.

But he was wrong. I remembered the flash of color in the trees. The fishing line.

"The fisherman," I said. **"The hermit fisherman."**

CHAPTER 9

GONE FISHING

We cleaned up camp and Dad tied Boris up.
*I would have felt bad for Boris, except I don't think
he even noticed.*
Dad made the leash
long enough that Boris could sleep near the fire. Boris
thought that we made that fire just for him.

We cleaned up the mess tent, fixed the pole, and
set the chairs up again. Then Bec, Joe, and I had a
Secret Club meeting down near the stream.

"So what do you think?" I said.

"There's no way Boris made all that mess,"
said Bec.

We peered across to the other side of the river, but I
couldn't see anyone.

"Do you think he'll be back?" said Joe.

"Not while we're around," I said.

But what if the hermit fisherman came back to our
camp at night and **attacked us in our tents?**

"Maybe we should tell your parents," said Bec.

We argued about that for a while and finally agreed **it was the right thing to do.**

Back at camp, Dad listened to our story and shook his head.

"I understand you want to keep your dog out of trouble, but it's no use," said Dad. "I'm sure it was him. There were **paw prints on the floor** of the mess tent."

"But that could have been from before!" I said.

Dad held up his hand. "David, that's enough. Boris is staying on the leash."

We had hot dogs for lunch, so there were only a few dishes to wash. Harry and Joe had to help do the dishes, so Bec and I sat around the fire. I couldn't stop thinking about the fisherman.

We spent the rest of the day trying to catch fish for dinner. **First we had to find some worms,** which is harder than it sounds. We finally found some by lifting rocks and **DIGGING** a little in the dirt underneath.

Bec didn't want to use worms, so she put a crumb of bread on her hook.

Fishing wasn't very exciting. Dad taught us how to throw the line out into the deepest part of the water. It made a good plopping noise when the sinker dropped into the water, but the only things we caught were a couple of **twigs** and some old **tree bark.**

We all sat on the bank in the dirt with our lines in the water, except for Dad.

"I'm not getting muddy," Dad said.

I looked up at him. **He looked like he hadn't taken a bath in a week.** His face was ⅅℐℛ𝒯𝒴. His hands were ⅅℐℛ𝒯𝒴.

"My jeans are spotless," Dad said.

He was right. They were. *So he found a patch of green weeds to sit on.*

It seemed to me that fishing was just a whole lot of sitting around waiting for something to happen. I had one eye on my fishing line and one on the opposite bank.

I didn't think the **hermit fisherman** was nearby, but if he was, he wouldn't say anything with Dad there.

"Well, no fish for dinner tonight," said Dad.

Bec didn't seem too unhappy about that.

Back at camp, Mom had something BUBBLING in the pot over the fire. I couldn't believe I was hungry again.

"That's the outdoors for you," said Dad.

"What are you cooking, Mom?" I asked.

"Camp pot roast," she said.

After dinner, we roasted **marshmallows** on long sticks that Dad found in the forest. Harry couldn't get the hang of it. **He kept burning his marshmallows.** Bec was so good at it she had two sticks going at once.

After marshmallows, we settled down for the night. I was so tired I forgot to worry about the hermit fisherman. The sound of the tent zipper woke me up. For one crazy second, I thought it was the fisherman.

"David?" Mom whispered.

"What?" I mumbled.

"There's something wrong with your father," she said. "*I have to take him to the hospital.*"

It wasn't quite morning and it wasn't quite night. There were still some stars in the sky but some birds were stirring in the trees.

Inside my parents' tent, Dad was covered in a red rash. **He had huge lumps all over his body.**

"He's got a headache, too," said Mom. "I just don't know what's wrong. I need to get him checked out by a doctor. But I can't take everyone with us. There's not enough room in just one car."

"How long will you be gone?" I asked.

"It's about 45 minutes back to the nearest town," said Mom. "Hopefully there's an **emergency room** there."

"We'll be fine here. You just go," I said. "Bec, Joe, and I are old enough to take care of ourselves. We'll be okay."

"I'll take Harry, then," Mom finally agreed.

Harry was still ASLEEP. When Mom
tried to wake him, he rolled over and
buried his head under the pillow.

"Maybe I'll just let him sleep," Mom told me.
"I'm not sure what else to do. I'll leave a note at the
ranger's hut on the way. **He can keep an eye on
you.**"

"It'll be fine, Mom," I said.

"Can you watch Harry, David? You have to keep
an eye on your brother. I don't want him to wander
off." Mom sounded really upset.

"You can count on me, Mom,"
I told her.

I wish I had never said those words.

CHAPTER 10

WHERE'S BORIS?

I didn't go to sleep after Mom and Dad left camp. I watched Mom's car bounce back up the path we'd come in on. I pushed around the coals in the campfire and put some sticks into it.

By the time the others had woken up, I'd toasted some bread over the fire and filled up some cups with juice. The ice in the car fridge had melted and the juice wasn't as cold as it could be, but it still tasted okay.

I told them about Dad. **Harry** thought it might have been something Dad ate. **Bec** thought it might have been something Dad touched. **Joe** thought that Dad was just **faking it** so that he could go back to town to use a real bathroom.

When it was time to wash the dishes, I told Harry it was his turn. Harry said it wasn't his turn and that **I wasn't the boss of him anyway.** I said Mom had made me the boss, so he had to do what I said.

Then Harry stomped back to his tent and said he wasn't talking to me.

"Fine," I said.

"Fine," he said.

Joe, Bec, and I played another game of Monopoly. By the time we got 𝓑𝓞𝓡𝓔𝓓 of it, the sun had climbed high in the sky.

I kept waiting to hear the sound of Mom's car driving back. Instead, there was just the sound of the birds.

"Where's Harry?" said Bec suddenly.

"In his tent," I said.

"Where's Boris?" said Joe.

My stomach jumped to my heart then dropped to my toes. Boris was gone from beside the fire.

"Harry," I called out. "Harry?"

Harry wasn't in his tent.

"Maybe he's down at the stream," said Joe.

We rushed down to the stream.

Mom would kill me if she knew that I'd let Harry go to the stream by himself. But **Harry wasn't there.** And neither was Boris.

"We've got to find him before Mom and Dad get back," I said. *"They're going to kill me."*

We left a note for Harry that said he should stay at the campsite if he came back. We left it on the picnic table, held down by a tin cup.

"Don't worry, we'll find him," said Bec as we headed off.

But of course we didn't. **And then we got lost.**

And that is where this whole story began.

CHAPTER 11

THE HERMIT FISHERMAN

When we realized we were walking in circles in the woods, **Bec wanted to just sit and wait for help.**

Joe wasn't sure what to do. I wanted to find the stream. I thought if we could find the stream, we could follow it back to camp.

"My plan will work," I said. "I've got a really good feeling about it."

"What if we end up back here?" Joe said.

"Then at least we've tried," I said. I lifted the backpack onto my back.

"We could drop cookies as we go," suggested Joe. "That way we could find our way back here if we don't find the stream."

"This isn't a fairy tale," snapped Bec. "Who do you think we are? Hansel and Gretel?"

"Wasn't there a house made of candy?" asked Joe. "That would be nice."

I headed off along a path as Joe and Bec argued about who would be Hansel, who would be Gretel, and **who would be the witch.**

We plodded along. The path seemed to go DOWNHILL. The trees towered on either side of us.

Every now and then we'd call out Harry's name, but there was **no answer.** I hoped Mom and Dad weren't back at camp.

We'd been walking for about ten minutes when the path seemed to end. There were NO SIGNS to tell us where to go.

"Now we're really lost," said Bec.

"We're just as lost as we were before," Joe said.

"No, before we were just lost," said Bec. "Now we're really lost."

I was looking at the trees, trying to figure out if I knew where we were, when I noticed **something strange** about the bushes on my left.

They looked brown and dead, unlike the bushes around them, which were green.

I went over to the brown bushes, picked them up, and moved them away. The  bushes were covering the entrance to a CAVE. I grabbed the flashlight from my backpack and shined it inside.

"Hey," I shouted. **"Look what I found!"**

Bec and Joe rushed up behind me and looked inside.

"COOL," said Bec.

"WOW!" said Joe.

"I'm going in," I said.

The cave started out low. We crouched down and squeezed our way inside.

Suddenly the ceiling lifted and we could stand up straight. There was a wide rock ledge on one side and a narrow rock ledge on the other. There was something on the narrow ledge. I couldn't tell what it was.

When I took a closer look, it turned out to be a small box holding a tin mug, a plate, and a fork.

"Artifacts!" said Joe.

"David, shine your flashlight on the wall," said Bec. "I think I see something."

I swung the flashlight around the cave walls and stopped on a spot farther inside the cave.

"What is that?" said **Joe**.

"Some kind of **painting**," I said.

The painting looked new. It was a picture of a **fish**. The scales were shiny greenish blue, and its eye was bright yellow.

I moved farther into the cave. "Come on," I said.

"I don't know if we should," said Bec.

But I didn't listen. I just kept moving. **The cave narrowed into a tunnel.** Then the tunnel widened out into another cave. The ceiling was higher there. I swung my flashlight around to see what I could see.

The flashlight showed another painting on the wall. This painting was older than the colorful fish in the first cave. The colors were dull and faded. The man in the painting looked like he was spearing a large animal.

"Oh!" said Bec.

I knew how she felt. *The painting seemed ancient, older than Mom or Dad. Even older than Gran.*

"This is AMAZING," I said. "Wait until we tell someone about this. We'll be famous! Wait until Rose Thornton sees us on TV."

For a moment, I'd forgotten all about my lost brother. Then a voice rang out from the tunnel.

"Hey!"

It wasn't Harry.

I turned off the flashlight and we stood silently in the dark.

I thought about bears, but I figured **bears couldn't talk.** So it couldn't be that.

Something was *breathing* heavily near my ear. It was Joe.

"**Who's there?**" yelled the voice.

I would have known that voice anywhere. It was the hermit fisherman. I'd known it would come to this. He would kill us and leave us in the cave.

No one would find us. Maybe hundreds of years from now they'd dig up our bones.

A thin beam of yellow light pointed into the tunnel. It grew BRIGHTER as it got nearer.

Then the flashlight shined on the three of us huddled together. The voice said, "Oh, it's you."

I turned on my flashlight and shined it back at the voice. It was a guy with a fishing rod dangling from one hand.

He looked about the same age as my sister Zoe. And he didn't look scary at all.

"What are you doing in here?" he demanded. "This is my place."

"Your place?" I said.

The fisherman told us his name was **Matt**. Matt lived with his dad right in the park. Matt's dad was the ranger.

"Did you **trash our camp**?" asked Bec.

"Yeah, what was that about?" asked Joe.

"What?" said the fisherman. "What are you talking about?" He seemed PUZZLED. I guessed Boris must have been to blame after all.

"What are you doing here?" Matt asked.

"We're looking for someone," I said. "My brother, Harry. He's been MISSING for hours."

"Was he the little kid throwing rocks the other day?" asked Matt.

I nodded.

"I saw him half an hour ago. He was at the stream near your camp. He was with a dog, and he said he'd been looking for you," Matt said.

I couldn't believe it.

"I'm going to kill Harry when I see him," I muttered.

"He was with some other people," Matt added.

"Other people?" said Bec.

"Yes," Matt said. **"He called them Mom and Dad."**

CHAPTER 12

POISON IVY

Matt said he'd help us get back to our campsite
if we promised him something first. "It's about the
painting," he said.

"Did you paint the fish?" asked Bec. "It's
FANTASTIC!"

Matt seemed *embarrassed*. "It's about the other
painting," he said. "I haven't told anyone about it.
I didn't want people coming around and *wrecking* it."

"But **it doesn't belong to you**," said Bec. "Maybe
you should share it."

"Do you want to get back or not?" he asked.

He had a point. We promised not to say
anything about the painting.

Matt grabbed something that looked like a
phone out of his back pocket. It was a **walkie-talkie**.
"Matt to base, over," he said.

There was a **CRACKLE**. Then a voice came
through loud and clear. "Base to Matt, over."

"Yeah, have located **missing parties** and bringing them back now, over," Matt said.

"Roger that, Matt. Meet you at the Baxter campsite," the voice said. I guessed that it was Matt's dad, the ranger.

Matt showed us the way back to camp. **We couldn't have done it without him.** It took us about half an hour, and by the time we got back the sun was sinking behind the trees.

Mom and Dad were talking to a guy dressed in green. I figured he was the **park ranger**. He was patting Boris, who was still on the leash and still lying by the fire.

Dad still looked **red and blotchy** from his medical problem.

"How are you, Dad?" I asked.

"A bad case of POISON IVY," he said. "I think it was that **green patch** I was sitting on yesterday."

"Happens to people who don't know their way around the wild," said the ranger, nodding.

Dad frowned.

Mom looked red and blotchy for a very different reason. **I hate it when she gets mad.**

"David Mortimore Baxter!" she cried.

"Hi, Mom," I said.

I sat on a chair and took my shoes off. I had blisters on my blisters on my blisters.

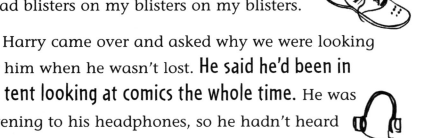

Harry came over and asked why we were looking for him when he wasn't lost. **He said he'd been in his tent looking at comics the whole time.** He was listening to his headphones, so he hadn't heard us. And he was hiding in his sleeping bag, so I hadn't seen him. When he got hungry, he came out. He found our note, so he stayed at the campsite.

The whole time Harry was talking to me, Mom was yelling about how **irresponsible** it was for us to leave the campsite.

What would Bec and Joe's parents think if she had to tell them their children were lost? What were we thinking? **And on and on.**

Then Dad asked the ranger and Matt to stay for dinner. Mom finally stopped YELLING at us. Then she disappeared into the mess tent to start cooking something for dinner.

"So, what do you think of camping, young man?" the ranger asked Harry.

"It's awesome," said Harry.

* * *

Back at school, everyone had a story about their spring break. Jake Davern went to the **zoo** three times.

Sam Beavis went to the **Football Hall of Fame** and had his photo taken with his favorite player. We were impressed until he told us that it hadn't been his favorite player in real life. It was a life-size picture of his favorite player.

Paul Jurkovic went SURFING with his dad and he stood up on a surfboard for a whole ten seconds before he fell off.

Rose Thornton kept very QUIET about her vacation.

"What did you do for your vacation?" I asked Rose.

"Wouldn't you like to know?" said Rose.

"Yes," I said. "That's why I asked you."

"Well, I'm not telling you," said Rose.

"Fine," I said.

"Just so you know, it wasn't a stupid camping trip. That's for sure," said Rose.

"Yeah," one of Rose's friends piped up. "A trip to your grandma's house is way better than a stupid camping trip."

Rose turned bright red.

Ms. Stacey told everyone to settle down. Then she held a newspaper clipping up for us to see.

The article said that **an ancient cave painting** had been found in Blue Hill State Park.

The press was keeping the location SECRET. They needed to protect the painting so that no one would damage it.

The article also said that a park ranger's son had found the painting.

"Now, isn't that a surprise, after our discussion about artifacts?" said Ms. Stacey.

But Bec, Joe, and I weren't surprised at all.

About the Author

When Karen Tayleur was growing up, her father told her many stories about his own childhood. These stories continued to grow. She says, "I always enjoyed the retelling, and wanted to create a character who had the same abilities with 'bending the truth.'" And David Mortimore Baxter was born! Karen lives in Australia with her husband, two children, two cats, and one dog.

About the Illustrator

Brann Garvey grew up in the great state of Iowa, where he studied art and visual communications. He graduated from the Minneapolis College of Art & Design with a degree in illustration. Brann is usually found with one or more of the following: a pencil in his hand, a comic book, a remote for watching DVDs, or his pet kitty, Iggy. When the weather is nice, Brann likes to play disc golf, and he proudly points out that Iowa is one of the world's centers for the sport. Iggy does not play.

Glossary

ancient (AYN-shunt)—very old

artifact (ART-uh-fakt)—an object made by human beings, especially something used in the past

campsite (KAMP-site)—a place where tents are set up

canvas (KAN-vuhss)—a type of coarse, strong cloth used for tents, sails, and clothing

equipment (ih-KWIP-muhnt)—tools or materials needed for a particular purpose

gear (GEER)—equipment and clothing

hermit (HUR-mit)—someone who lives totally alone and away from other people

inspect (in-SPEKT)—look over something very carefully

irresponsible (eer-ee-SPON-suh-buhl)—careless, without a sense of responsibility

ranger (RAYN-jur)—someone in charge of a park or forest

revenge (ri-VENJ)—action that you take to pay someone back for harm done to you

wilderness (WIL-dur-niss)—an area of wild land

Discussion Questions

1. Why doesn't Matt want to tell anyone about the cave paintings he found? What would you do if you found an ancient artifact?

2. Why do you think David's dad wanted to go camping so badly? What are some of the ways his behavior changed?

3. David and his friends go fishing and on hikes while they're camping. What are some other things you can do in the wilderness?

Writing Prompts

1. Has your family ever gone on a special trip or vacation? Write about it. Where did you go? What did you see? Did you have fun?

2. Has there ever been a time when you were left in charge and something went wrong? Write about what happened and what you did to fix the problem.

3. In this book, lots of David's friends go on different vacations during Spring Break. Write about a dream vacation you would like to take. Where would you go?

David Mortimore Baxter

David is a great kid, but he has one big problem — he can't stop talking. These wildly humorous stories, told by David himself, will show readers just how much trouble a boy and his mouth can get into, whether he's going on a class trip, trying to find a missing neighbor, running a detective agency, or getting lost in the wild. David is amiable, engaging, cool, and smart enough to realize that growing up is the biggest adventure of all.